When the Dentist Came to School

Carmel Reilly
Photographs by Lindsay Edwards

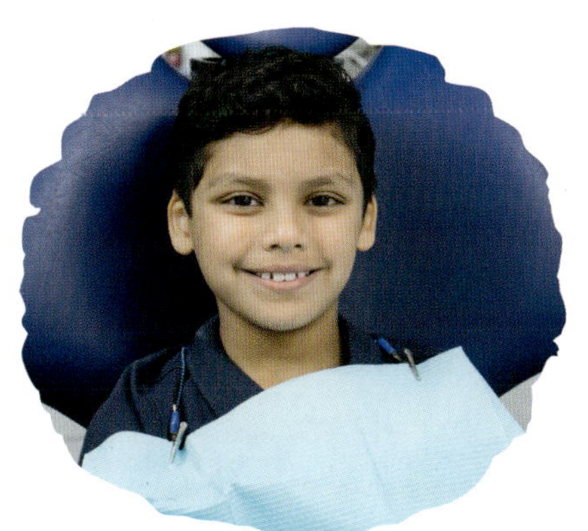

Contents

A Dentist in a Van

Today, I went to see
a **dentist** at school.

This dentist was not like other dentists
I have seen before.
He came to school in a van!

The van had a room in the back
where the dentist saw the children.

Dometic

It was my turn to see the dentist
in the afternoon, just after lunch.

As I waited by the door of the van,
I looked inside.

I could see a big chair
in the middle of the room.
Beside the chair, there was a little table
with the dentist's **tools** on top.

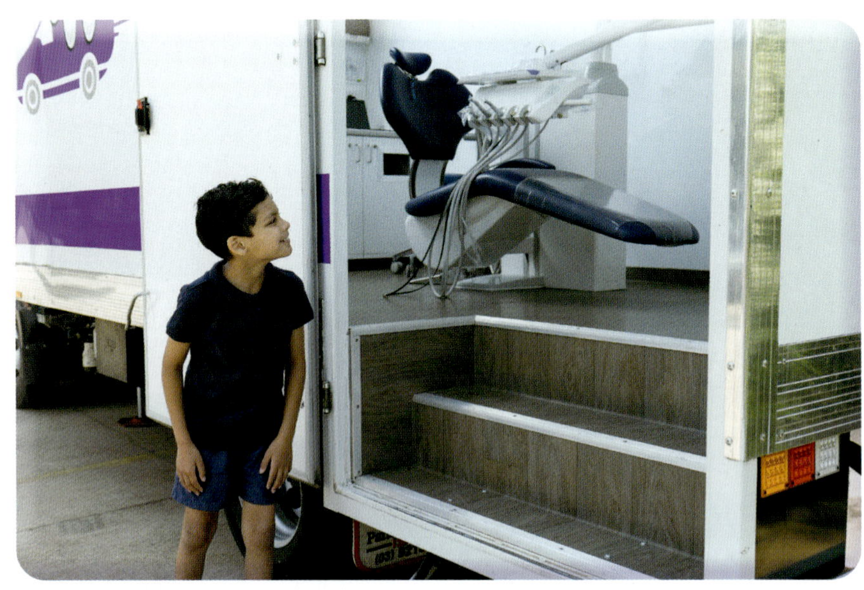

Soon, the **nurse** called me inside.

She told me that her name was Tessa,
and that the dentist was called Rami.

Rami gave me a big smile.

Then, Tessa asked me to sit down
in the big chair.

When I was ready,
she put a **bib** around my neck.

DIPLOMAT

Open Wide

Rami gave me some glasses to put on.
Then, he tipped the chair back
so that he could see inside my mouth.
Next, he turned on a big light above me.

Then, Rami picked up a tool from the table.
He asked me to open my mouth wide.

Rami looked at the teeth
at the back of my mouth.
Then, he worked his way
around to the front.

He told me that I had done a great job
of taking care of my teeth.

All he had to do now
was to clean them.

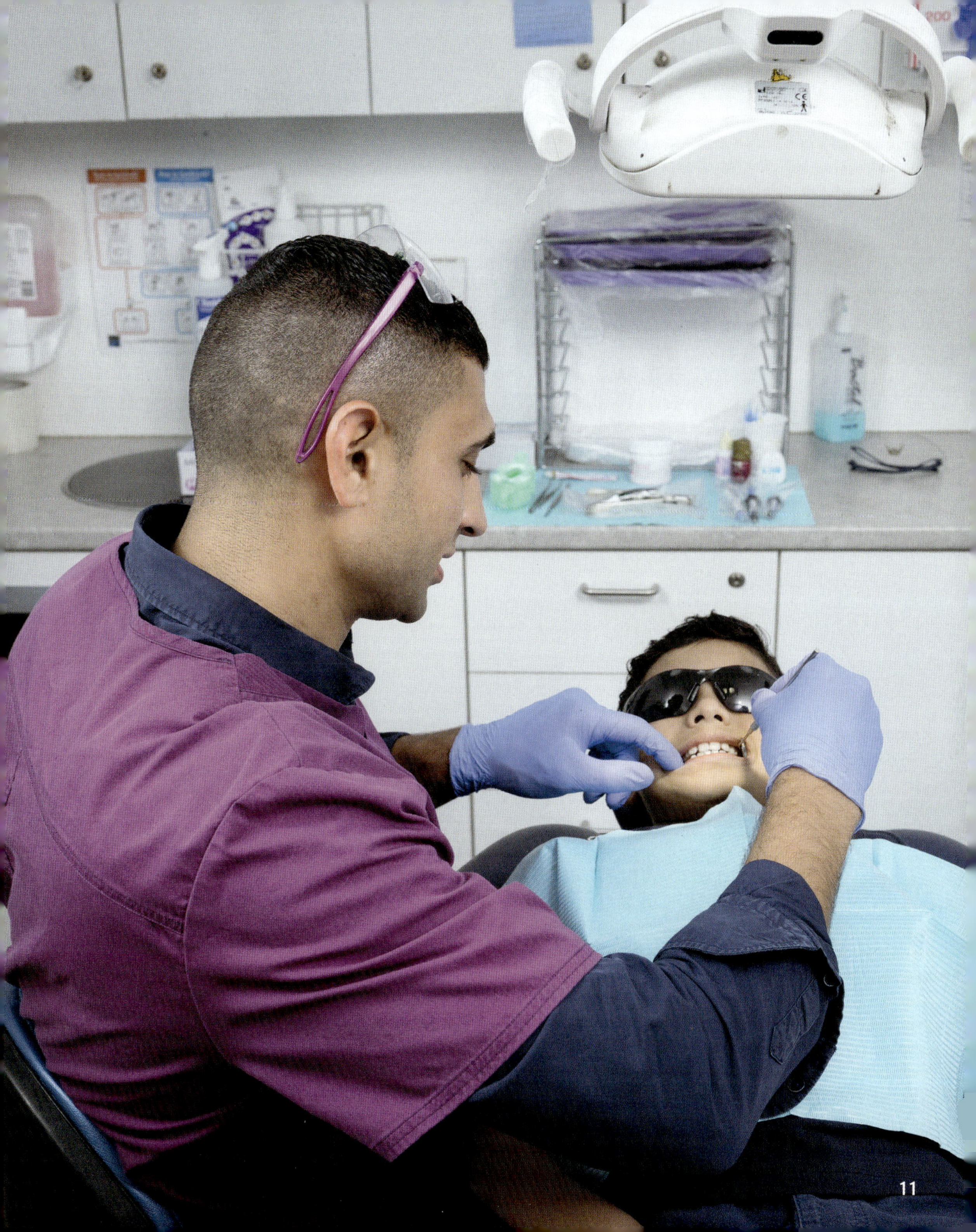

Rami picked up another tool
to clean my teeth.

I asked him if cleaning them
was going to hurt.

He said that cleaning could sometimes
feel a little funny,
but it would not hurt me.

Keep Up the Good Work!

After Rami had cleaned my teeth,
he put the chair back up.

As I got off the chair,
Rami told me to keep up the good work.

I went back to the classroom
with a big smile on my face.

It was great seeing the dentist
in the van.

Glossary

bib something that goes around your neck to cover the front of your clothes

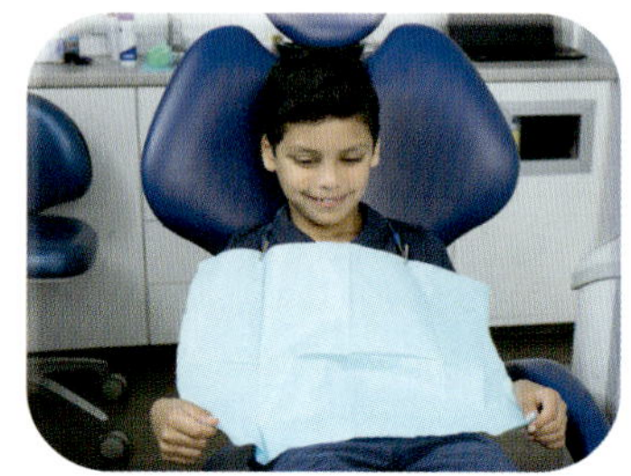

dentist a person who looks after your teeth

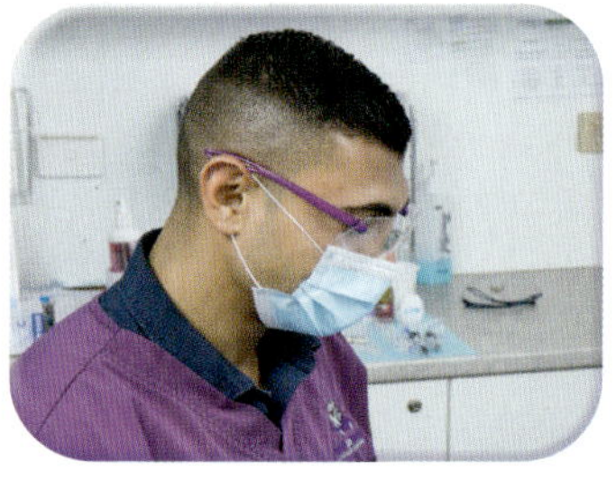

nurse a person who helps the dentist

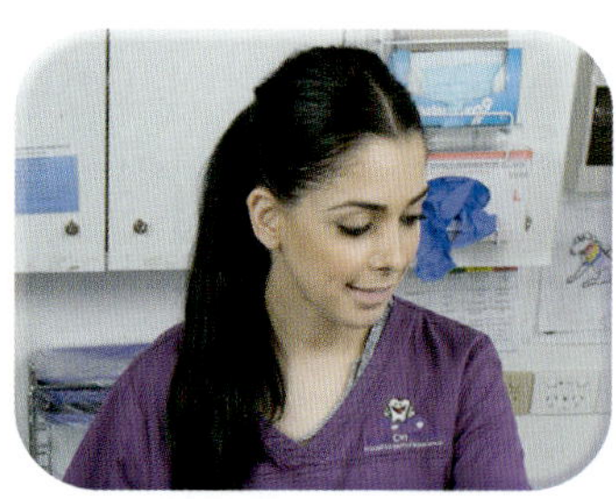

tools things to help do a job

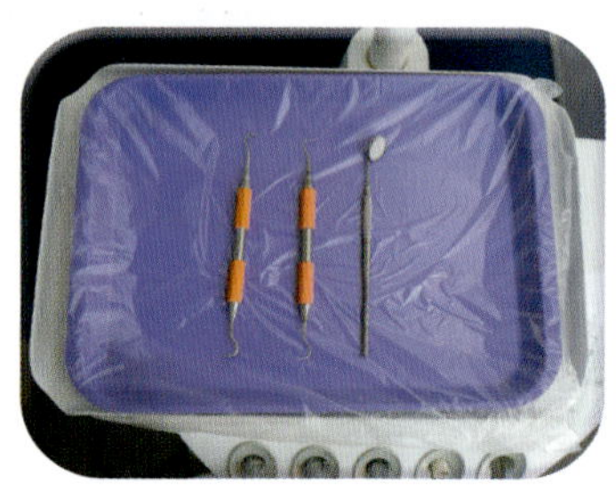